701

P9-BVG-822

The Finest Christmas Tree

John and Ann Hassett

Houghton Mifflin Company Boston 2005

Walter Lorraine Books

For Grampa Martin

Walter Lorraine Books

Copyright © 2005 by John and Ann Hassett

www.houghtonmifflinbooks.com

Library of Congress Cataloging-in-Publication Data

Hassett, John.
  The finest Christmas tree / John and Ann Hassett.
       p. cm.
  "Walter Lorraine books."
  Summary: After Farmer Tuttle is unable to give his wife a Christmas hat
because he cannot sell his Christmas trees, he receives a mysterious letter
requesting his very finest tree.
  ISBN-13: 978-0-618-50901-0 (hardcover)
  ISBN-10: 0-618-50901-1 (hardcover)
[1. Christmas trees—Fiction. 2. Christmas—Fiction. 3. Santa Claus—Fiction.
4. Hats—Fiction.] I. Hassett, Ann (Ann M.) II. Title.
  PZ7.H2785Fi 2005
  [E]—dc22
                                                    2005000557

Printed in Singapore
TWP 10 9 8 7 6 5 4 3 2 1

The Finest Christmas Tree

Farmer Tuttle was a Christmas tree farmer.
His forest was full of pointy-topped trees.
Children liked to hear the chop of his ax and
the cheery putt-putt of his tractor.

Every Christmas
Farmer Tuttle
piled the trees onto his
truck for a trip to the city.
He sold his trees from a
busy street corner. He
helped shoppers pick a
tree that was just right—
not too big and not too
small.

When all his trees were sold, he shopped
at the city stores for a special gift.
Farmer Tuttle always bought Mrs. Tuttle
a new Christmas hat.

oh what fun it is to ride in a one horse open sleigh...

But one Christmas, shoppers did not stop to buy
Farmer Tuttle's trees.
"Smart shoppers want trees made of plastic," said a man.
"Plastic trees are positively perfect," a lady said.
"Plastic trees go back in the attic till next Christmas,"
said another.
Farmer Tuttle piled his trees back onto the truck.
There was no money to buy Mrs. Tuttle a
new Christmas hat.

Farmer Tuttle
did not go
into the forest
anymore.

13

The next winter, a man from the sawmill
offered to buy all the trees in the
forest. He wanted to saw the trees into
toothpicks and clothespins. The man
gave the Tuttles until Christmas to decide.

Farmer Tuttle wondered what to do. Then, with only one day till Christmas, a strange letter came in the mail. It read:

Dear Farmer Tuttle,
  The workers at our
  factory wish to have
  the finest tree in the forest
  for their Christmas party.
  A crew of cutters
  will arrive shortly.
  Season's greetings,
    The Boss

Farmer Tuttle hurried home with the happy news.
He waited all that day. He waited long into the night,
but the crew of cutters did not come.
"Perhaps they have chosen a plastic tree," he said
to Mrs. Tuttle. He began to think about toothpicks
and clothespins. Farmer Tuttle tugged on his hat
and coat, and he set off for the forest.

Farmer Tuttle was surprised to find small footprints in the snow. He scratched his puzzled head. Paths of tiny footprints wandered from tree to tree all through the forest.

Soon Farmer Tuttle heard the
chop-chop of an ax.
He saw a tall, pointy-topped tree
fall to the snow.

Tiny figures rushed to the tree. They lifted it to their small shoulders. They trotted quickly over the frosty ground and tossed the tree onto the back of a sleigh.

25

Little voices cheered
as the sleigh raced
over the snow. It
leaped over the treetops.
Up and up the sleigh
flew through the
silent, glimmering
stars, and then it
was gone.

Farmer Tuttle found a box where the tree
had stood. Inside was a beautiful Christmas hat.
He tucked the box under his arm and
hurried home.

Farmer Tuttle's trees still grow in the
forest. Every year at Christmas, the crew
of cutters returns for another finest tree.
Children have seen the tiny footprints
in the snow. And Mrs. Tuttle always
gets a new Christmas hat.